Love from Angelina

Illustrations by Helen Craig Based on the text by Katharine Holabird

PUFFIN

Angelina loves . . . dancing with her friends at Miss Lilly's Ballet School.
Angelina dances everywhere! She loves spinning, twirling and leaping.

Dancing makes Angelina
very happy, but dancing
isn't the *only* thing
Angelina loves.

Angelina loves . . . her best friend, Alice.
Angelina and Alice like to do all the same tricks,
like cartwheeling round and round
the playground.

Alice knows how to do some things better than Angelina – like perfect handstands.

But Angelina never stops trying, even if she takes a tumble on the playground grass and the other mouselings laugh.

Luckily, Alice is a good teacher.
She is patient with Angelina and
gives her lots of encouragement.

With Alice as her partner,
Angelina learns to do a
perfect handstand.

Angelina loves . . . the fair. But it's hard to do all of her
favourite things when little cousin Henry comes along.
Angelina loves soaring through the air on the big
wheel – but Henry hates the big wheel.

Angelina loves zooming up and down the roller
coaster – but Henry hates zooming up and down.
Angelina loves the dark and twisty turns in the Haunted
House – but Henry hates anything dark and twisty.

Still, when Henry wanders off
without her, Angelina gets
very worried.

Then, when Angelina finds Henry again,
she remembers what she loves even more
than big wheels and roller coasters.
She loves her little cousin Henry.

Angelina loves . . . riding her bike with Alice
down bumpy country roads.

When the road gets
a bit *too* bumpy . . .

. . . Angelina is especially glad to
have her good friend by her side.

Angelina loves . . . ice skating. Before the big
ice-skating show, Henry needs a little extra help.
Angelina and her friends let him hold their tails so
that he won't fall down on the slippery ice.

But how can they practise
when Spike and Sammy
keep bothering them?

Angelina learns that Sammy loves
doing funny tricks and that Spike
can skate backwards . . .

. . . so she asks them to be in the show. She
knows that if all her friends work together,
the show will be better than ever!

Angelina loves . . . to work hard and to do her very best.
But things don't always go her way. When Angelina
falls ill before an important rehearsal, she's much
too dizzy to dance. Poor Angelina!

Angelina is very
disappointed, but when she
feels better, she decides to try
again. And this time, she
dances beautifully.

Angelina loves . . . her family.

She loves the comfort of her mother's arms when she's feeling ill or sad or even angry.

She loves the sound of her father's fiddle. When he plays for her, she feels like a real ballerina.

And she loves dancing for Grandma and Grandpa. They are the very best audience!

Angelina loves . . . her baby sister, Polly. Being a big sister isn't always easy. Polly gets lots of attention and Angelina has to try very hard not to get jealous.

Polly tries to do everything that
Angelina and her friends can do,
but she's too little. So Angelina
holds Polly and promises her
that some day, she'll teach her
how to dance and do tricks,
because . . .

. . . that's *just* what Angelina loves.

You make
me dizzy!

Friends
forever!

We have fun
together!

Be mine?

With love

To: _____

From: _____

With love

To: _____

From: _____

With love

To: _____

From: _____

With love

To: _____

From: _____

Let's dance!

You make me feel like dancing!

I love hanging out with you!

Happy together!

With love

To: _____

From: _____

With love

To: _____

From: _____

With love

To: _____

From: _____

With love

To: _____

From: _____

You make
me dizzy!

Friends
forever!

We have fun
together!

Be mine?

With love

To: _____

From: _____

With love

To: _____

From: _____

With love

To: _____

From: _____

With love

To: _____

From: _____

Let's dance!

You make
me feel like
dancing!

I love hanging
out with you!

Happy together!

With love

To: _____

From: _____

With love

To: _____

From: _____

With love

To: _____

From: _____

With love

To: _____

From: _____

You make
me dizzy!

Friends
forever!

We have fun
together!

Be mine?

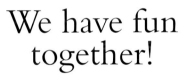

With love

To: _____

From: _____

With love

To: _____

From: _____

With love

To: _____

From: _____

With love

To: _____

From: _____

Let's dance!

I love hanging
out with you!

With love

To: _____

From: _____

With love

To: _____

From: _____

You make
me dizzy!

Friends
forever!

We have fun
together!

Be mine?

With love

To: _____

From: _____

With love

To: _____

From: _____

With love

To: _____

From: _____

With love

To: _____

From: _____